Overcoming
LAZINESS

Learning to make an EFFORT

Jasmine Brooke

FOX EYE
PUBLISHING

Crocodile loved to **REST**.
He liked to **RELAX**.

He enjoyed taking it
really **EASY**. He took
his **TIME**. He loved being
LAZY – all day long.

Crocodile loved nothing
better than doing ...

2

4

On Monday, Mrs Tree asked everyone to write about their weekend. Parrot had a lot to say. She was always **BUSY**.

Zebra started scribbling. She was always on the **GO**.

Rhino got to work. He was always **CHARGING** about!

But Crocodile **LAZILY** looked out of the window. He decided to take it **EASY**. He decided to take his **TIME**.

But **TIME** ticked by, and by the **TIME** the lesson ended, Crocodile had written **NOTHING**. Not a word.

Mrs Tree gave Parrot a star. She had **WORKED** so hard. Zebra got a badge. She had really **TRIED**. "Well done," Mrs Tree told Rhino. "Great **EFFORT**."

Crocodile was **JEALOUS**. Maybe he should have **TRIED**. Maybe, just a bit.

9

At football practice, everyone really **TRIED** their best. **QUICKLY**, Lion took the ball. Monkey **JUMPED** high to kick it.

Turtle **TUMBLED** in her shell to pass the ball.

But Crocodile just took it **EASY**. He decided to take his **TIME**. When Turtle passed the ball to him, he didn't even **TRY** to score. Not one bit.

Mrs Tree gave Lion a star. He had **WORKED** so hard. Monkey and Turtle got a sticker. They had really **TRIED** too.

Crocodile was **JEALOUS**. Maybe he should have **TRIED**. Maybe, just a bit.

Crocodile shuffled from side to side. He didn't like how he felt. Not one bit.

Mrs Tree had been watching Crocodile. She took him to one side. "Taking it **EASY** doesn't always feel **GOOD**," she said. "It can feel **BETTER** to **TRY**. Even just a bit."

Crocodile shuffled from side to side. He knew that Mrs Tree was right. More than a bit.

"I think it's time to **TRY**," Mrs Tree said. "See how **THAT** feels."

The next day, Crocodile **TRIED** in the lesson. He **WORKED** hard at football practice too. Crocodile got a badge. He even got a star.

Crocodile grinned from ear to ear. **TRYING** felt great – much more than just a bit!

From then on, Crocodile **TRIED** in everything he did. He had learnt that being **LAZY** made things hard, and that didn't feel great. Not one bit!

Words and feelings

Crocodile was very lazy in this story and that made things difficult.

LAZY

EASY

There are a lot of words to do with being lazy and working hard in this book. Can you remember all of them?

WORKED

TRIED

EFFORT

Let's talk about behaviour

This series helps children to understand and manage difficult emotions and behaviours. The animal characters in the series have been created to show human behaviour that is often seen in young children, and which they may find difficult to manage.

Overcoming Laziness

The story in this book examines issues around laziness. It looks at how being lazy can cause problems for people, and how it can also create issues for those around them.

The book is designed to show young children how they can manage troublesome feelings and behaviours, and how they can help others to deal with feelings and behaviours, too.

How to use this book

You can read this book with one child or a group of children. The book can be used to begin a discussion around complex behaviour such as laziness.

The book is also a reading aid, with enlarged and repeated words to help children to develop their reading skills.

20

How to read the story

Before beginning the story, ensure that the children you are reading to are relaxed and focused.

Take time to look at the enlarged words and the illustrations, and discuss what this book might be about before reading the story.

New words can be tricky for young children to approach. Sounding them out first, slowly and repeatedly, can help children to learn the words and become familiar with them.

How to discuss the story

When you have finished reading the story, use these questions and discussion points to examine the theme of the story with children and explore the emotions and behaviours within it:

- What do you think the story was about? Have you felt lazy when you have been asked to do something? What was that situation? For example, were you asked to tidy up but did not want to? Encourage the children to talk about their experiences.

- Talk about ways that people can cope with laziness and tools they can use to help them to apply effort. For example, people can think about how they will feel when they have accomplished a task or a reward they may receive as a result of doing something. Talk to the children about what tools they think might work for them and why.

- Discuss what it is like to cope with the disappointment that may result from laziness. Explain that Crocodile was disappointed in the story because he did not receive a prize when the other animals were rewarded for trying hard.

- Talk about why it is important to work hard and try your best when carrying out a task. Discuss the value of doing so.

Titles in the series

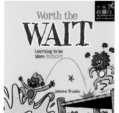
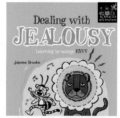

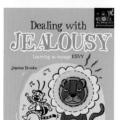

First published in 2023 by Fox Eye Publishing
Unit 31, Vulcan House Business Centre,
Vulcan Road, Leicester, LE5 3EF
www.foxeyepublishing.com

Author: Jasmine Brooke
Art director: Paul Phillips
Cover designer: Emma Bailey & Salma Thadha
Editor: Jenny Rush

All illustrations by Novel

ISBN 978-1-80445-291-2

A catalogue record for this book is available from the
British Library

Printed in China